FABLES FROM THE HOLLOW:

"THE GREAT SING"

A story for children of all ages based on
the teachings of Bhagavan Sri Sathya Sai Baba

by
J.F. Ziegler

Illustrated by
J.F. Ziegler and P.L. Blackwood

Copyright 1986 by Joy Ziegler

Published by Hallelujah Press Publishing Company,
P.O. Box 496, Gilbert, Arizona 85234-0496
Library of Congress Number 95-43719
ISBN 0-9621235-1-X

Acknowledgements

As I sit alone putting the final touches on *The Great Sing* before it goes to press, I realize each friend who worked toward the completion of this book came to me separately and stated, "I want to dedicate my time and effort on this project to Sai Baba. I want nothing in return." And so I shall only thank Bhagavan Sri Sathya Sai Baba for sending me Laurie Shepard, Patti Blackwood, Ronne Marantz, and James and Susan Coulbourne, for without their devotion and service, this book might still be a dream.

A word from the editor

After twenty-five years of working with children in a public school setting, I have come to realize the importance of quality literature which teaches life's important values. It was a privilege to help Joy with a book which brings these qualities to children. It is my sincerest hope that children will receive Sai Baba's message which is implicit in the pages of this book.

Susan Coulbourne

Dedication

This book is dedicated to Sri Sathya Sai Baba who taught me "There is only one caste, the caste of humanity. There is only one religion, the religion of love. There is only one language, the language of the heart. There is only one God, and He is omnipresent. Let the different faiths exist. Let them flourish. And let the glory of God be sung in all the languages and in a variety of tunes."

With Love and Blessings
Sri Sath Sai

INTRODUCTION

Fables from the Hollow, "The Great Sing" is a unique blend of Eastern philosophy and Western story-telling. A saga that is rich in character and parable, the plot extols the path of right action. *Fables* is a significant story steeped with thought-provoking ideas and filled with timeless truths. Fascinating characters take the young reader on a journey that is fun and inspiring. This non-violent fantasy is traditional in the sense of good overcoming evil, love replacing hate, and giving becoming more important than taking. Service to others is the stuff the heroes are made of. Imaginative and enlightening, this story launches the reader on a journey to the real "Self" -- to the place where dreams are born and peace of mind is king.

The Great Sing

Table of Contents

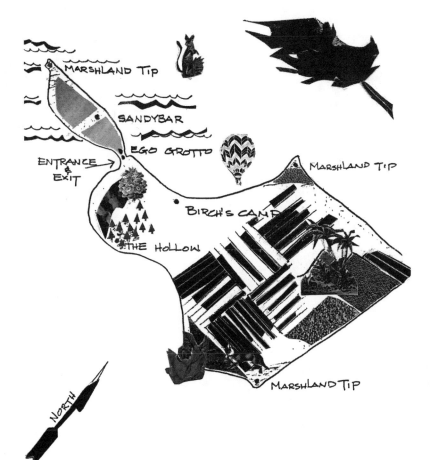

MARSHLAND TIP

SANDYBAR

EGO GROTTO

ENTRANCE
&
EXIT

MARSHLAND TIP

BIRCH'S CAMP

THE HOLLOW

MARSHLAND TIP

NORTH

Only One Entrance

CHAPTER 1

Birch Visits the Hollow

When the wind stopped, the seed fell. Born in the warm, fertile soil of the Hollow, it began to develop. If you were keen on nature things and looked very closely, you might notice its head peeping out from the rich earth. As the days turned warm, then cold, and then warm again, the small seed grew into a lovely young flower.

There is a structured society in nature, much like the one we use as human beings. Nature has her leaders, householders, communicators, teachers, mothers, fathers, and so on -- all equally important in the chain and structure. The Hollow also lived by the laws of nature. Sometimes the laws were cruel. Only the fittest survived and, unfortunately, the strongest were

1

not always the wisest.

Birch, the sheriff of the Hollow, was cruel and unhappy; although he was a most awesome birch. Nature had made him strong and tough. However, it wasn't his height that made you step back and take notice. It was his lopsidedness. The arms on the right side had long ago been chopped off, and only the stubs remained to tell of past dangers. The left side of Birch was full of arms with leaves aplenty. Many arms could extend deep into the Hollow itself. Birch appeared unusual because of the overabundance on one side, and the barrenness on the other.

He frightened the residents of the Hollow. Birch was the law! Discrimination, or knowing the difference between right and wrong, was not part of his character. He looked for the bad in everything. No one had ever seen Birch smile, or even wrinkle, or pucker around the mouth, in an almost smile.

Life went on in the Hollow. After all the planning, the wedding of Mr. Evergreen to Miss Pine Cone was finally over.

The Hollow Council met as usual on Tuesday nights. Church began on Sunday mornings at nine o'clock sharp.

The Plantfolk were a likable sort -- hardworking, God-loving, family-oriented types. All those, that is, except Birch's guards. Like their leader, they only found the bad in everything and showed no kindness to anyone, not even their own.

About noon one day, towards the end of the week, Birch's guards were seen 'round town tacking up notices. After they left, the Plantfolk went to reading. The notice posted said, **"ANYONE CAUGHT BEING HAPPY WILL BE PUNISHED."** by order of Birch's law.

The new law caused great sorrow among the inhabitants of the Hollow. They were a happy group. To stifle happiness was great torture. Love, happiness and service to others were a way of life in the Hollow. To stifle these feelings would lead to eventual death.

A secret meeting was scheduled among the community leaders. Those involved that night were a serious group.

Conducting the meeting was young Mega Maple. It seemed natural, too, that he should lead. A handsome stocky tree, the others always turned to him for advice and courage. He was standing a very short step or two from the seed born earlier in the story. Her name was Blossom.

Old Crow, who always sat in the arms of Gideon, the ageless fig tree, was present. There was Euripides, a tall, thin eucalyptus; Jolly, the large oak; Gnat, a small tree with odd-shaped leaves; a mulberry named Hume; a vine, reddish in color, whom the others called Vinny; and the old pine, known simply as Wise. These were the leaders of the community. Their motives were to serve.

The Fig was speaking, "Why, to be unhappy is a sin against life." The others nodded in apparent agreement. "Happiness, or peace of mind, is a gift from the Great Spirit. To pretend otherwise is...is...is, I'd rather be reincarnated," Gideon finished.

"Why is Birch against happiness?" questioned Blossom.

4

The Town Meeting

Gideon seemed to want to reply, and the others let him. "Time past, seasons and seasons ago, Birch was unhappy. Some say the wind made him that way, and others say it was the Great Flood. The old-timers, they don't say. From what I know, it centers around his lopsidedness. He was quite handsome once," he explained.

The others squirmed in disbelief. Birch, handsome? They had trouble picturing him that way.

Gideon continued, "One day, towards the end of winter, a human came to the Hollow. With a gleaming ax, he cut the arms off Birch to use for firewood. Things have never been the same since, and they are getting progressively worse. Birch never rallied nor regained happiness. That's as true a tale as you're going to get. I was young then, but it's something I'll always remember," Gideon finished.

"That would be hard to take, but to see no happiness in anything is far worse than what happened to him," observed Gnat.

"What are we going to do?" questioned Vinny the Vine.

Wise, the old pine, spoke softly and gently, "The one weapon to use against hate is love. Only by our example of love, by our right action, will we overpower Birch. Love is the greatest force in the Universe." Wise cleared his throat and continued, "We must realize happiness is inside of us, not something to be found outside, or taken away. Our hearts can be happy, our actions can be good, our thoughts kind, but a smile never has to cross our faces. This may fool Birch," he concluded.

"What a terrible way to live," mused Hume.

Euripides cried out, "Why is this happening to us?" Panic was evident among the Hollow leaders, so powerful was Birch's hate.

Finally, Mega spoke, "We must do as Wise advises. At least for now. There is no other way. We have a township to worry about, not just ourselves. I know it isn't much; but, it is a beginning, something to hold onto."

Vinny Is Caught

There was grave concern in everyone's hearts when the meeting ended. As the others left for home, Mega and Blossom stood speaking. Everyone knew flowers and trees didn't mix socially. It was generally thought to be a waste of time to get involved with a flower. That was the fashion in those days. It didn't bother either one of them.

CHAPTER 2

Vinny Smiles

Morning arrived and the community was alerted to the plan -- smile in the heart and mind, but not with the lips. Hopefully, this would pacify Birch. The town was strange, to say the least. No one was singing, and faces were without smiles. The Hollow suffered silently.

Birch appeared at noon, roving the streets for anything good to ruin. He passed Gnat's place, then Hume's. Entwining his way through the streets, Birch stopped close to Blossom. "You're a pretty, young thing," he boomed. "Too bad you're a flower."

Nervously, Blossom looked up, making sure not to smile as she did so.

"Who Are You," Hissed Agni?

Birch left and continued his walk, finishing at the Hollow's entrance. The tundra-foliage types breathed a sigh of relief. The plan had worked. Everyone was safe ... for now.

Blossom and Mega continued to see each other, even though there was no future for them together. Rules were rules. Two different species just didn't mix, not in the Hollow. It was unheard of for a tree and flower to be friends. It was another problem for the residents of the Hollow to be concerned about. Rules and laws without truth as a foundation are not things upon which to base values. So besides having to smile in the heart, not on the face, the folks of the Hollow had to worry about Mega and Blossom, and a law no one understood.

Birch continued to enforce his new law, and the days passed, frightfully and slowly. Then, the inevitable happened. Vinny got caught with a smile on his face, a sign of happiness, punishable by law! Vinny was taken to Birch's camp and held prisoner.

A second meeting was called in the Hollow. All were present, except Vinny the Vine. Mega looked worried, as he called for quiet in the meeting. "Truth will never let us down," he began. "We must continue to smile in our hearts, though our faces be grave. These great tests come often in life. We must not quiver or deviate from what we know as right."

Looking down, seconds passed as Mega gathered himself together. Speaking again, he said, "We will find a plan to release Vinny. A good plan. One where no one is hurt. We must teach Birch to love!" he wailed, and slumped back.

The others all started talking at once. How to teach Birch to love? That was the urgent question they all pondered that tense night in the Hollow.

Old Crow flew about nervously, listening here, talking there. The moon was asleep. It was dark. Hume the Mulberry took the floor. "We could write him a letter and tell him we love him," spoke Hume. "But, I believe actions are better than words; words are easy to say, easy to come by."

Ego Grotto

"How to act to reach Birch?" he reflected out loud to himself. Still holding the group's attention, he paused, then continued, "Anger and hate are born out of fear and hurt. Deep pain. Perhaps this pain makes it hard for Birch to open his heart and love, or forgive and forget."

Jolly interrupted here, and the Mulberry sat down. "What about giving Birch gifts? This might soften him up a bit, eh? We could all give him something of value." Before he could go any further with his suggestion, Wise stood up and said strongly, "Gifts! Buying gifts in the name of love. I'm sorry, Jolly, but you can't buy love. It is given of the heart. Love lives in everybody's heart. Like Hume said, the heart feels frightened and locks up. We must find the key to Birch's heart and unlock it. We must think," he concluded.

Mega picked up where Wise left off. "You speak of value, Jolly, giving something of value. What is valuable to you may hold no value for me. The real valuables are good character, honesty, kindness, love, service. You can't gift-wrap

11

these and give them away. You earn these treasures. You don't have to dig them up, or use a map to find them. You find them within. Know thyself. Who are you? Where are you from? Where are you going when this life is called back? The answers to these questions are the greatest gifts of all. The answers give peace of mind. What greater treasure is there, than peace within? No, we must find another way."

And so it went through the night. Someone throwing out an idea, another testing it. Dawn found them much closer to a plan than the previous dusk.

The Love Attack

CHAPTER 3

A Secret Visit to Birch's Camp

Mega arrived, with Old Crow, to secretly visit Vinny at Birch's camp. They waited until it was fully dark the following evening.

The night was chilly. Vapor floated from their mouths as they whispered. They were overwhelmed by the size of Birch's camp. Mega stepped into a large shadow cast by an old building. Old Crow flew about in search of the imprisoned Vinny. It was a long time before Old Crow came back and spoke with Mega. Then they set off toward the north, careful not to alert anyone to their presence.

An ugly wire net held Vinny captive. Startled to see Mega and Old Crow, Vinny stifled a scream. Mega greeted Vin and then told him of his family and their well-being. The Hollow folks had pitched in. Each had brought an item or two for Vinny's family. Consequently, a nice pantry had been set up for his Mrs.

Old Crow told Vinny of the daring plan to rescue him. He then produced a bag of food for Vinny to hide for himself. Mega said they would return soon. Vinny was brave. The others were scared.

Mega and Old Crow scouted the camp after leaving Vinny, taking notice of anything that would make their bid for him a little easier. They returned to the Hollow.

The days were filled with torment because of the NO HAPPINESS LAW. To conceal joy for life was a strangling experience, and the Hollow continued to suffer. The children were kept silent. Laughter brought reproach from parent or adult. Business collapsed. There was no reason to go into town. You couldn't gab with anyone about anything for fear of being happy. Activity was kept at a minimum. Folks only did enough to get by. They were surviving, not living. The NO HAPPINESS LAW caused two more to be taken away before the plan to rescue Vinny could be put into action. Now there were more to worry about. The Hollow dwellers were slowly, and sadly, losing the happiness from their hearts. Something had to happen soon, or....

Old Crow, Gnat and Hume were talking about the fighting among the Hollow folks. Arguing among friends was becoming commonplace. Anger was quick to surface, and forgiveness slow in coming. The Hollow was dying.

The NO HAPPINESS LAW was to blame. It must be stopped. Eventually, there would be no one but Birch, and happiness would never again be heard of. Through the layers of history, it would be lost, forgotten as something of the past.

Mega called another meeting. As the evening dampness reached up around them, the group was clearly restless. He began to tell of unity and faith in each other and in all things. The night deepened. Euripides, the tall, thin eucalyptus,

15

reminded, "If we don't work together, we are surely doomed." He sounded self-assured. He also mentioned the relationship between Mega and Blossom. They had been so helpful to the Plantfolks in the Hollow. All are brothers after all, regardless of species.

The town meeting seemed long. The tension was mounting. The plan was scheduled to begin the following day. Piping hot food in large amounts was offered after the meeting. Drinks of fresh juice and coconut milk were colorful and refreshing.

Mega came forward and began to speak, while the others feasted. "Eat," he said, as he smiled. "Relax, enjoy this life God has given to you." His words were like a tranquilizer. It had been weeks since the law was posted, and no one had really relaxed since. Euripides tripped over his own thin limbs, and everyone laughed at this. A lot of food was eaten that night in the Hollow, and a lot of coconuts were drained. Music filled the air, as the hummingbirds played favorite after favorite.

Mega, Pine and Old Crow then gathered in the corner, deep in conversation. Old Crow slipped off unnoticed. Later he reappeared and flew directly over to Mega and Pine.

Nodding together, Pine stood up. He stepped forward. "Excuse me," he said, and waited to receive everyone's attention. He finally began to talk. "I don't have to tell you of the hard times that have come to the Hollow. One wonders why life brings sorrow to one, happiness to another. I don't know the answers. But I do know that God never gives us more than we can handle. I also know all that happens, ultimately, is the Will of the Spirit. There are reasons beyond our comprehension for what happens. We must trust in the One. Thoughts, as you well know, hold great power, and energy follows thought. The next 36 hours will be critical to our plan. It is imperative that we erase the negative thoughts from our minds and send only thoughts of love, not only to Vin and the other captives, but to Birch also."

As Pine expected, this last statement brought rebuttals

and comments flying towards him. Pine waited patiently until the initial outburst had subsided, and he began again. "We must start to trust one another as before and trust ourselves. We have lived all these years in the Hollow and always included the Spirit in our lives."

Pine drank some juice and continued, "Since the NO HAPPINESS LAW, we have forgotten the good and only focused on the bad. That's not how we are used to solving our problems in the Hollow. Is it?"

A few no's echoed through the Hollow in reply, and heads signaled in agreement with Pine. He then continued, "Our blessings are many." He lowered his voice, as if to tell a secret. Everyone strained forward to hear.

"This is the plan."

Long after the others had gone home, Old Crow, Pine and Blossom continued to perfect the plan. The key to Birch's heart is love. The basic plan was to love Birch's heart open and unlock it with love. A daring plan indeed! To love one as mean and intolerant as Birch was, well, nearly impossible. Vinny and the rescue were another matter. This was a touchy problem.

CHAPTER 4

Termite Joins the Rescue Team

Gophers and the tundra-foliage types did not get along. Gophers were notorious for their love of tundra-foliage for nourishment. Because of this, they were considered mortal enemies of the Hollow....

Later the same evening, another meeting took place in the Marshland, the southern tip of the Hollow. Mega and the most feared of all the gophers, Termite, were deep in discussion. The water from the Marshland was cold. Mega was nervous, and beads of perspiration dripped from his leaves.

Termite's teeth gleamed as he spoke to Mega. "What is in this for me if I help spring Vinny and the others from Birch's camp?" His teeth flashed.

Mega waited a few moments before speaking. What he was about to say, and how he said it, were of utmost importance. He began slowly and seriously. The success of the rescue rested on this moment.

"Service to another is what's in it for you; there is no other reward than that. The Holy Scrolls tell us to forget self, and by forgetting self, we become desireless. By becoming desireless, we acquire peace of mind. What greater reward, Mr. Termite, is there?" questioned Mega.

Without waiting for a reply, he continued, "If you serve and don't seek the fruit of your action, no Karma will beset you. So to help you, for your own benefit, I will let you serve our Hollow." Mega paused, then started again slowly, "Of course, I can offer this service to another."

Termite could wait no longer. "I'll do it, I'll do it. Now cut the mush, and let's get on with it before my good sense tells me to do differently."

Mega told Termite of the plan to use his teeth to cut

away the wire cage, so Vinny and the others could go free. The gopher was astounded, but kept silent.

Slipping back to the Hollow, Mega reported his positive conversation to the others. They were pleased. Mega and Termite were to meet at the Cave's entrance at midnight. Now all everyone could do was wait and hope.

Phase one of the plan was on schedule. Mega and Termite found each other by the Cave's entrance. Taking care to be quiet, the two made their way to Birch's camp. To be caught meant death.

A guard was making his nightly check. He coughed deeply and blew his nose, then resumed walking. Termite and Mega knelt close to the ground before moving out into the open. They listened intently. All was quiet, except for the soft breeze. Cautiously, they made their way to the prison. Stopping again, they hugged the earth, peering into the darkness. Remembering Vinny's near fatal outburst from his last visit, Mega told the gopher to stay put. Termite agreed and sat down, idly touching his teeth.

Mega approached the wire cage and called softly, "Vin, Vin, it's me, Mega." Again he called. No answer. Mega moved closer and repeated his previous message.

This time Vinny whispered, "Over here, Mega, I'm at the other end."

Mega crawled over and spoke to Vinny, "Termite's here, Vinny, he's with me now. Are you ready?"

"Yes," gulped Vin.

"Then tell the others," ordered Mega.

Vin could not believe his life was dependent on the gopher, one of the Hollows's greatest enemies. How life dips and changes, he thought, waiting there in the silence. An enemy come to save an enemy. Perhaps Pine and the others were right. Maybe the real importance was in matters of the heart.

Stealing away, Mega found Termite asleep in the shadows nearby. "Termite, wake up, the time is here," Mega urged, as he gently poked him in the stomach. The gopher responded with a yawn and stretched awake.

Termite hopped onto the wire net and began to chisel with his teeth. It was slow going, and Mega wondered if time would be their enemy, too. Termite had to finish before the sun woke up. Maybe they should have started earlier.

Vinny and Mega were sweating, despite the chill. Pulling and pushing the wire, they heaved to and fro with every pass of the gopher's teeth.

"Birch's guard," hissed Vinny. "He's making another check."

Mega was hidden before Vin finished the sentence. Termite stopped in mid-saw and knelt down. The guard was so close, they could smell his cigar. Vinny stifled a cough. The guard would not leave and stood facing the net, drawing on his smoke. Termite held his breath, and at last, the guard strolled to the other end of camp.

"How much time has that cost us?" wondered Mega, as

he resumed work with the others.

It seemed like hours had gone by before a hole in the wire could be seen. Stooping to get a closer look, Mega and Termite leaned forward with such force, they fell through the hole and deep into a crevice. Luckily, the other two prisoners were on guard at the south end of the net and were only knocked down from the force of the earth's opening.

The momentum easily carried Vinny along with Mega and Termite. A floor had opened in the bog. Down, down, down, down, they tumbled, finally bumping to a stop somewhere in the nether regions of the world. Gasses seeped around the rocky earth, leaving a smell that was pungent and nauseating. The heat made breathing difficult.

Feeling along the ground as he spoke, Mega choked to Vinny and Termite, "Where are you?"

"Over here," Vinny whispered back.

Termite was beside himself. He could not believe what he was involved in. "I'll never dig out of this place," he said to

25

himself, touching his teeth worriedly.

Fire bathed the room, eating everything it was hungry for. Flames reached out like arms. The fire spoke, "I am Agni. Who are you?" The booming voice lisped, as flames leaped everywhere.

Mega, Vinny and Termite said not a word.

Again the authoritative voice repeated the question, "Who are you?"

Fighting back the fear, Mega made a brave attempt to speak, but nothing came out.

Instead it was Termite's voice that was heard through the crackling fire, calling to Agni. "Sir, I'm Termite, most feared of all gophers. Over here is Vinny the Vine and this is Mega Maple."

Turning the pages of his checklist that was bound with leather, trimmed with bone, Agni stated rudely, "You are not on my list. You can't be in Hell."

Rushing to a shelf containing thousands of books, bound

in the same way, uniform in size, he seized the one on the very top row.

"Let's see," he leered, flipping through the pages of the small book, "Where are you supposed to be?" His voice made the earth move, and gasses hissed with the motion.

Mega, Vin and Termite the Gopher sat huddled together. Agni grimly continued to search. The heat was unbearable, the smell sickening.

"You can't be in Hell! Get out of here, you'll ruin me!" Agni bellowed, reading from the book. "You're good and kind, honest and forthright. I can't tolerate those characteristics. They make me ill," he slobbered.

Hands of heat held Vinny, Mega and Termite. The flames were brilliant, as they smothered the endless pit.

Agni questioned the intruders sharply, "Your thoughts are too pure, your actions too kind to bring you to Hell. How did you get here?" he breathed hotly.

Again it was Termite who responded. "We were serving

27

another, and the ground beneath us opened like a door. We fell down, down...."

Before he could finish, Agni swelled to full strength and burst disgustingly, "Serve another, serve another!"

Then sucking like a hurricane, Agni pulled Vinny, Mega and Termite forward without effort and regurgitated them upward with great force. The heat disappeared as the trio traveled at split second speed. Up, up they flew, and the smell of gasses followed them. Moss grew abundantly. It was dark and green and damp. They continued to surge upward....

CHAPTER 5

Sandybar & Great Uncle Faraday

When Mega did not return at the appointed hour, Old Crow, Wise and Blossom began to wonder. Sensing a mishap, they waited breathlessly for word of Vinny, Mega and the others, but none came.

A new sense of confidence had filled the Plantfolk since the night before. The voice of Wise filled their minds, and his speech of the previous night lingered in their thoughts. It had been a great inspiration. Remember? 'Trust one another, trust the Spirit, love all things, for all is really One. We've always included the Spirit in our lives....'

Remembering the speech was a source of great strength for the Hollow inhabitants, and the Plantfolks worked with ease.

29

Everyone was relaxed. The tension had dissipated like steam.

Birch's Law didn't bother those in the Hollow this day. They didn't even think about it. "Minimize what you don't have; maximize what you do have; serve others; forget self; become desireless." All breathed these thoughts throughout the Hollow. The fear of Birch was forgotten. He was thought of with love, as the plan indicated. They waited patiently for the return of their friends.

When Mega, Vin and Termite regained wakefulness, they were on a beach. The sand that surrounded them was wet, and the air was sultry and thick.

"Where in the name of the Holy Scrolls are we?" inquired Termite. Vinny and Mega were considering the appropriate reply. Since there was no one else, they each felt compelled to answer Termite's question. After all, it was because of them that Termite the Gopher was in this strange place.

"Old Crow! Old Crow!" shouted Mega excitedly,

breaking the silence. The others saw the bird and began to yell also. The Crow responded to the shouting, circling and landing neatly among the three lost friends.

"Why, I'm not Old Crow," he said, laughing. "I'm his Great Uncle Faraday; nice to meet you. What are you doing in these parts? Not many visitors up this way, too dangerous. What are you folks doing here?" he asked again.

"Where are we?" questioned Mega. "And then I'll tell you what we're doing here."

"You're in Sandybar," answered Faraday. "Not many folks...."

"Sandybar!" interrupted the three visitors in unison.

"No one is brave enough to live in Sandybar," said Vinny.

"Oh, there are a few," replied Faraday wisely. "What brings you here?" Faraday again asked.

Mega answered this time. "Birch is killing the Hollow. He's posted a new law: NO HAPPINESS; and anyone caught smiling is subject to punishment. The folks are brave, but to remain unhappy this length of time is slowly killing us.

"We went in rescue of Vinny the Vine and two others. Termite the Gopher here," Mega motioned towards the gopher, "was using his teeth to cut the cage where Vinny and the others were held captive. The ground gave way under our weight and the force of our work."

Faraday nodded silently.

"We fell through some kind of a door in the earth. The heat was oppressive as we traveled past layer upon layer of rock. We arrived in Hell, but we were released after being questioned by Agni."

Faraday interrupted here. "Why were you released?"

"Our goodness," stated Mega briefly. He then continued, "We were hurled upward; the heat turned icy; the smell was heavy and gassy; and we woke up here, Mr. Faraday. I'm so worried about the Hollow," Mega finished with a sigh.

"I can gain entrance to the Grotto and guide you back," offered Faraday.

Vinny and Termite spoke for the first time, "Thank you, thank you, Mr. Faraday."

Mega silenced them with his hand. "That is nice of you, Mr. Faraday, but I'm already responsible for Termite the Gopher being here. I don't want to be responsible for you, too."

Faraday smiled and replied, "Son, I appreciate your point, but the One will take care of old Faraday. His Will be done. I am an answer to your prayer, am I not?" he inquired gently.

"Yes," said Mega softly, "You are. And we would be glad to let you serve us," he reconsidered. Vinny and Termite, the most feared of all gophers, smiled and nodded enthusiastically.

They were going home. Faraday said he would have to stop at his home before leaving for the Hollow. When he returned, he had a welcome bag of warm food and drinks.

With the moon in full dress, wearing stark white clouds with puffy sleeves, the night appeared hazy. Refreshed, Mega,

Faraday and the others started towards the Grotto that would allow entrance to the Hollow. As they walked at a steady pace homeward, Mega told Faraday of the plan to love Birch's heart open.

CHAPTER 6

Ego Grotto

Back in the Hollow, a day had come and gone with no word of Mega and the others. The Plantfolk were determined in their efforts to ward off Birch with love. Never did they think a negative thought about anyone. With steadfast minds, they praised the One within and were happy. With great faith, they knew their friends would return; and with great hope, they prayed for mean Birch.

It was voted upon by the Hollow residents to send out a rescue party of one to trace the disappearance of Vin, Mega and Termite. Old Crow was chosen. Gideon, the ageless fig, saw him leave. Crow was calm and self-assured, as he soared high. Stretching his wings, he made a wide arch and headed toward the Marshland tip.

Faraday, Mega, Vin and Termite were close to the passage that allowed entrance to the Marshland and the Hollow.

"This is the most dangerous area of Sandybar," informed Faraday. "Because of this passage, the area is deserted."

"Why, it's beautiful," said Termite the Gopher. "What is the reason?" he wanted to know, waving his hand towards the lush grass and sandcastles sculptured by the wind.

"In order," replied Faraday, "To get to the entrance and exit of Sandybar, Marshland and Hollow, you must pass through Ego Grotto. The pull upon the senses, the illusion of only self, are a nightmare. Few return once they enter the Grotto. The senses are strong and uncontrolled. They have stamina, and the ego is sneaky. One desire is fulfilled, another springs up. It is a vicious cycle. It is endless, and eventually you are playing so fast, you can't get out," said Faraday knowingly.

Termite asked the unavoidable question, "How do you

know so much about Ego Grotto, Mr. Faraday?"

Faraday, showing agility younger than the title "Great Uncle" indicated, turned around to face Termite and the others. If you looked closely, you could see the gray feathers around his beak that were the only giveaway to the number of years he'd lived. "I was once part of it," Faraday confessed.

"How did you get out?" questioned the gopher again. "You said you couldn't."

"I know," replied Faraday seriously. "I started thinking good thoughts, and I ignored the pull of my senses. I started to love others as I love myself, and I began to put self aside in order to serve others. My desires lessened; and with that, the senses became bored, but only for a moment. However, it was long enough for me to escape. I never wanted to go back. Nevertheless, I have gone back, but only for the most auspicious reasons," he finished.

Silence followed. Vinny finally spoke, "How do you get out again, when you go for auspicious reasons?" He waited for

37

a reply.

"That is the secret I will share with you now; but it can only be used in service for humanity, or it will not work." He began to tell them the key to the great mystery.

"I enter Ego Grotto calmly," he stated. The others were breathless with anticipation, eager to learn the secret that would save them. "I walk with equanimity to the center of the Grotto. It is ugly. You can see all through yourself. There is no hiding. I stand, and I ask confidently, 'Who are you, senses?' I wait. There is no answer. I yell again, 'Who are you, senses?' I wait again. Still there is no answer. I continue to walk peacefully towards the opening. There is still no comment. They have no power over me. I am neither the senses nor the ego. I am part of the One -- The Great Spirit. I go to the entrance/exit door. There is a knock from outside. It is fear. With faith, I open the door, and no one is there. I leave. It is the same way to go back," he finished knowingly. The others were eager to enter.

As Old Crow's Great Uncle Faraday had predicted, Ego

Grotto was demanding, repulsive and distorted. Also, as Faraday had forewarned, the senses held no answer to the inquiry, 'Who are you?' The quartet ventured further inside the Grotto, and a foul smell filled the air. Vision was impaired, as self blinded the eyes. Still they trudged on.

Good thoughts filled their minds. The senses pulled upon the travelers and made a bid for permanence. "Come over here, this way; no look over here," cried the Ego. The group fought hard and continued toward the south. Their ears were burning with sounds of the senses. A greasy substance clung to the walls of the Grotto. As they approached the door, the knock Faraday warned of earlier occurred, and they were ready. It would be fear. With faith, Mega answered the door. It opened with a squeak, and cobwebs fell away. No one was there.

CHAPTER 7

The Attack

Old Crow instinctively headed for the Sandybar area. Even knowing he might be swallowed by Ego Grotto, he still continued his search. Flying low, then high, he scanned the Marshlands for his friends. Hours passed.

Finally, he spotted them traveling towards the Hollow. Delight filled Old Crow, as he circled low to greet them. "Hello there! Hello!" he called. Faraday saw him first and pointed skyward. The others followed his wing with their eyes.

Landing neatly, Old Crow shook hands all the way around. "Uncle Faraday, what are you doing this side of the Grotto?" Even though he already knew the answer, Old Crow waited for the older crow to speak.

"I'm just being," replied Faraday, not willing to mention his lifesaving effort to help the Hollow residents return home. Able to contain himself no longer, Mega asked about the township. "Old Crow, Old Crow, what is happening in town with Birch?" he interrupted.

"Calm down, old buddy, everything is fine." Relief filled Mega and the others. "The Hollow dwellers are strong in their determination, and the town is coming back to life. Even with the NO HAPPINESS LAW in force, the folks are thinking positively," continued Old Crow.

"What about sending the love thoughts to Birch? That is an important part of the plan," Mega stated.

"All thoughts are love thoughts. The whole town is working to help Birch," finished Old Crow with a smile.

"Good," nodded Mega, the stocky young maple.

Moving slowly, Vinny, Old Crow, Mega, Faraday and Termite the Gopher drew closer to the Hollow. Time went by rapidly. The sun told Faraday and Old Crow the day was growing tired. Shadows grew long, as the bright ball worked its way west. The hours passed. It wasn't far to the Hollow now, and Old Crow and Faraday flew ahead to scout.

Stopping near the Hollow entrance, the tired group waited for Old Crow and his uncle to return. The ivy that covered the Hollow entrance was thick and hid them well.

Faraday and Old Crow returned to warn the others that Birch was on his way to the Hollow. This was it! The time had come. The plan had to work.

Old Crow left again, this time to warn the Hollow dwellers that Birch was coming. Faraday remained with the others. Old Crow flew with great speed.

Slipping into town, he gave the urgent message to Gideon and Wise. Euripides and Hume were waiting, too. The signal was then given to Blossom. Moments later, the residents of the Hollow were alerted, yet not a word had been spoken.

Each one's position for the love attack on Birch was of the utmost importance. Acoustics were essential. Hume and

Euripides rolled the bomb cannon into position. Gnat and Jolly saw the children to the hideaway; safety was assured there. Others discreetly did their assigned jobs. Birch would soon be there, and they had to work fast and carefully.

Mega, Vinny, Termite the Gopher, Old Crow and Faraday entered the Hollow unseen. Silently, they prepared for Birch's arrival. They each had a task to do. Mega loaded the cannon and set the aim. Gideon positioned the altos; Wise, the tenors; and Euripides was in charge of the sopranos. The inhabitants of the Hollow were ready.

As he entered the Hollow, the sneer on Birch's face was hideous. Ignorance guided him; and hate filled him, twisting his expression into one of contempt. He looked rumpled and unclean, as he walked toward the center of town.

"Now!" yelled Mega. The Hollow dwellers responded at once to Mega's command. Beautiful vibrations filled the air, instantly penetrating Birch's heart. Rhythms danced through the Hollow, and a chorus of golden voices sang harmoniously.

43

Altos, tenors, sopranos, all blended into one serenade to Birch.

Mega lit the cannon that held the love bomb gently inside its womb. Wow! Ignition! Love exploded everywhere! The love cadence continued from the chorus and cannon. The Hollow dwellers never stopped -- not for dinner, not to open shop, not to play. Those who could not sing, hummed. Everyone helped.

At last, Birch could stand no more. Responding to the love, he smiled. Love occupied Birch's heart. The key fit; his heart was open at last. The hatred dissolved!

CHAPTER 8

Changes in the Hollow

There were changes in the Hollow, after "The Great Sing." Birch became kind, because he knew he was loved and because he started to love himself. Euripides became a father. Gideon aged another year; and Wise grew more intelligent. Termite the Gopher was honored as a timeless hero; and Great Uncle Faraday returned to Sandybar to serve and aid others through Ego Grotto. Blossom and Mega started a new fashion, as Gideon had predicted long ago. They were married in the spring. To this day, they are still wed. Old Crow turned gray. The Hollow flourished, and the children grew into caring leaders.

The wind blew steadily, then stopped suddenly, and a seed dropped in the warm, fertile soil. Another soul was born to the Hollow.

The End

STUDY QUESTIONS

CHAPTER 1   _QUESTIONS_

1.   Why was Birch unhappy all the time?

2.   Why were the leaders of the community good leaders?

3.   Why did Wise the old pine pick love as the weapon to use against Birch?

CHAPTER 2   _QUESTIONS_

1.   Why did Mega want a plan to release Vinny without harm to anyone?

2.   What is peace of mind?

3.   Can you name something that makes you feel at peace?

CHAPTER 3   _QUESTIONS_

1.   Why was the Hollow suffering?

2.   Pine told the Plantfolks at the meeting that God never gives a person more than he can bear. Can you share a time when you felt burdened, and Baba was there to help you shoulder the burden?

CHAPTER 4   QUESTIONS

1. Why did Mega tell Termite there was no greater reward than service?

2. Life is full of change. Vinny the Vine was aware of this when the gopher, his enemy, came to save him. Can you name some changes in your own life?

3. Mega, Vin and Termite fell into Hell. What do you think Hell is? Where do you think Hell is?

CHAPTER 5   QUESTIONS

1. When Great Uncle Faraday asked the three visitors why they were released from Hell, Mega's answer was brief. Can you explain why he did not talk more about himself?

2. Can you tell about a time when you put a friend before yourself?

3. How did it make you feel to put someone before yourself?

CHAPTER 6   QUESTIONS

1. The townsfolk had great faith. What do you think faith is?

2. Write two sentences using the word faith.

1.   What bhajans would you sing to open Birch's heart?

2.   Why did Birch smile?

3.   Can you name someone you love who at first was hard for you to love?

STUDY QUESTION ANSWERS

CHAPTER 1 - ANSWERS

1. He looked for the bad or negative in all things. He never smiled. As Swami teaches, there is only One and that One is God. Our thoughts make things beautiful or ugly.

    > "Bad thinking, bad seeing, and bad doing are animal qualities. By seeing bad things, how can you expect to get human qualities? Don't see bad things, don't do bad things and do not hurt anybody. Always be happy. Happiness is union with God."
    >
    > Sathya Sai Baba
    > Kodaikanal, April 11, 1991

2. Their motives were to serve others without thought of self gain. Swami teaches us to act as his instruments and never seek the fruit of our actions, but to dedicate all to God for all is God.

    > "All hands are His, all feet, all eyes, and all faces and mouths are His. He works through all hands; He works through all feet; He sees through each eye; He eats and speaks through each mouth. Everything is He. Every step is His; every look, every speech, every act is His. That is the lesson that service instills."
    >
    > Sathya Sai Baba
    > *Sathya Sai Speaks, Vol. VIII*, p. 15-16

3. Wise used love as a weapon because love is the only power that can make hate disappear.

"Nectar is described by the scriptures as extremely sweet. But nowhere does nectar approach the sweetness of love. Compared to love, nectar seems insipid. The uniqueness of such love is beyond the comprehension of ordinary people. Such love arises only when you churn the world of bliss...

"Acquire love through love, only through love can unity in diversity be experienced.

"Love, love, love. I love all and I ask all to love. My greatest wealth is love. People speak about My powers and My miracles, but love is my greatest miracle."

Sathya Sai Baba
Excerpts from discourse given at
Fifth World Conference
Hillview Stadium, Nov. 24, 1990

CHAPTER 2 - ANSWERS

1. It is never wise to hurt anything, for all is God.

"Inasmuch as ye have done it unto the least of these, My brethren, ye have done it unto Me."

Jesus Christ

"God is in every creature, so how can you give such pain?"

Sathya Sai Baba

"I am imminent in every being. People forget me as if I were without them. They are not aware that I am the inner core of every being. They are then tempted to believe that the phenomenal world is true. Pursuing worldly pleasures, they fall into grief and pain.

"If they would concentrate all attention on Me, recognizing that the Lord has willed everything and everyone, I would then bless them by revealing to them that they are I, and I am they."

Sathya Sai Baba
Sai Avatar, Vol. III

2.   Peace of mind is when thought, word and deed are in tune with one another. This produces harmony within when the thought is pure, the word truthful and the deed is done without ego and offered to God.

"The foundation for real peace is, according to the Vedas, the quality of my three. My three means amicability, compassion and kindness. It can also be taken to mean 'my three,' that is to say, my word, deed and thought shall be in accordance with thy word, thought and deed. That is to say, we shall speak, think and act together without friction or faction, in the atmosphere of love and understanding. That is what is wanted in the world today, My Three."

Sathya Sai Baba
My Baba and I, p. 161
Dr. John Hislop

1.   The Hollow was suffering because the townspeople had to hide their true feelings. Existence, Knowledge, Bliss. Swami teaches that our real Self is divine and always blissful as He Himself has demonstrated throughout His life. Even as a young boy He was made to suffer because some people who knew Him did not understand Him. Swami says that our real nature is Jnanaswarupa, the embodiment of Divine Wisdom.

> "Learn! Experience! Be Happy! It does not matter a bit if you have no faith in Me or in God. Have faith in yourself. That is enough. For who are you really? Each of you is Divinity, whether you know it or not."
>
> Sathya Sai Baba
> *Sathya Sai Speaks, Vol. III*

2.   Students relate stories.

> "God will grant you what you need and deserve. There is no need to ask, no reason to grumble. Be content, be grateful for whatever happens, whenever it happens. Nothing can happen against His will."
>
> Sathya Sai Baba
> *Sayings of Sathya Sai Baba*

> "Drapadi was once in great peril, and she urgently called upon the Lord to save her. He did so, but not until after some delay. She reproached Him, 'Lord, I called You, why did You take so long?' Krishna in turn asked, 'Where did you look? From where did you call

Me?' She answered, 'I called you from the residence in the capital city.' Krishna answered, 'Oh, that is the reason! I had to come from there to here. Had you called me from your heart, where I am always, I could have saved you without this delay!'"

Sathya Sai Baba
My Baba and I
Dr. John Hislop, p. 101

CHAPTER 4 - ANSWERS

1. Service to others helps to calm the mind. It takes you out of the "little silly self" and exalts you to selflessness. It turns the mind toward another rather than to one's own senses and the fulfillment of desires. Service to another is service to Sai.

    "Make every moment holy by filling it with loving service."
    Sathya Sai Baba

    "Each activity must be undertaken with the conviction that you are serving Sai in all forms."
    Sathya Sai Baba

    "Selfishness is the greatest negative tendency in human beings. Selfishness distracts the mind, disturbs the equilibrium, distracts perception and endangers progressive evolution. The six essential weaknesses -- lust, anger, avarice

(greed), attachment, pride and jealousy are only consequences of selfishness."
Sathya Sai Baba
My Baba and I, p. 170
Dr. John Hislop

2.   "You must have not only freedom from fear, but freedom from hope and expectation. Trust in My wisdom. I do not make mistakes. Love My uncertainty, for it is not a mistake. It is My intent and will. Remember nothing happens without My will. Be still. Do not ask to understand. Do not want to understand. Relinquish the imperative that demands understanding."
Sathya Sai Baba
Sanathana Sarathi, August, 1984

3.   Swami teaches that Hell is a tormented mind. Guilt, greed, and a lack of conscience contribute to make up Hell. Buddha speaks of Hell as a place.

"It is a place. A place of the mind. A mental state in which there is worry and suffering. It is an after death state. Sai is here to guide His devotees so they do not fall into that state."
Sathya Sai Baba
Conversations with Bhagavan Sri Sathya Sai Baba, p. 178
Dr. John Hislop

CHAPTER 5 - ANSWERS

1.   Mega did not let his ego take over because he was selfless. He passes over himself, concerned only for the folks living in the Hollow. The ego is anything that

makes you feel less than divine.

> "You can lay claim to be My devotee only when you have placed yourself in My hands fully and completely with no trace of ego."
> Sathya Sai Baba

> "Cut the 'I' feeling clean across and let your ego die on the Cross, to endow on you eternity."
> Sathya Sai Baba
> *Divine Memories of Sathya Sai Baba,*
>   p. 255
> Diana Baskin

> "To eliminate the ego, strengthen the belief that all objects belong to God and you are holding them in trust. This would prevent pride; it is also truth."
> Sathya Sai Baba
> *Divine Memories of Sathya Sai Baba,*
>   p. 243
> Diana Baskin

CHAPTER 6 - ANSWERS

1. Faith is surrender to God. Faith is acceptance of God's will. Faith is trusting in the Lord. Faith is the foundation of unquestioning belief.

> "God's power is like electricity and our bodies are like light bulbs. The light within can only be seen

when the switch of Faith is turned on."
Sathya Sai Baba
Living Divinity, p. 113
Shakuntala Balu

2.   Write two sentences with the word 'faith' in each sentence.

CHAPTER 7 - ANSWERS

1.   (Name bhajans)

"Singing the names of the Lord in a group of people will wean you away from distracting thoughts, whereas those thoughts will invade you when you do it alone. So sing aloud the glory of God, and charge the atmosphere with divine adoration."
Sathya Sai Baba

"You too must pass your days in song. Let your whole life be a bhajan. Believe that God is everywhere at all times and derive strength, comfort and joy, singing in your heart in His presence the Glory of God. Let melody and harmony surge up from your hearts and let all take delight in the love that you express through that song."
Sathya Sai Baba

2.   Birch smiled because he felt the love that surrounded him. Even sad and mean as he was, he realized someone loved him.

"Seen through the eyes of love, all beings are beautiful, all deeds are dedicated, all thoughts are beneficial, and the world is one vast family."
Sathya Sai Baba
Sathya Sai Baba's Divine Teachings
Grace Martin

WORD MATCH

Match the words in Column A with their meanings in Column B.

A	B
JOY	LESSON
TRUTHFUL	KARMA
DESTINY	SERVICE
HELP	LOVE
GOD	BELIEF
FAITH	HONEST
EGO	SELFISHNESS
FABLE	HAPPINESS
VALUES	QUALITIES

WORD SEARCH

Find the word and circle it. The words can be vertical, diagonal, and backward.

```
H  F  L  I  B  E  R  A  T  E  K  X  S
U  A  B  H  O  J  K  C  O  N  A  E  D
M  B  P  G  T  E  A  C  H  E  R  C  I
A  L  D  P  C  L  M  V  W  V  M  J  S
N  E  R  E  I  H  P  G  I  A  A  O  C
I  P  G  A  W  N  A  C  X  L  D  Y  R
T  H  J  C  J  D  E  K  O  U  L  D  I
Y  R  T  E  R  T  G  S  H  E  A  C  M
W  O  R  C  D  L  O  D  S  S  J  E  I
U  D  U  X  O  R  E  S  P  E  C  T  N
M  H  T  G  A  U  A  N  I  P  A  D  A
P  Y  H  O  L  L  O  W  R  G  Z  C  T
D  S  B  I  L  L  U  S  I  O  N  E  I
T  E  K  C  B  A  B  A  T  B  D  X  O
```

BABA	SERVICE	KARMA	HAPPINESS
OLD CROW	JOY	FABLE	TRUTH
EGO	SPIRIT	HUMANITY	PEACE
LIBERATE	HOLLOW	TEACHER	VALUES
RESPECT	ILLUSION	DISCRIMINATION	

60

GLOSSARY

Agni - Name of Hindu Fire God.

discrimination - To know the difference; to observe or note a distinction, as in favor of or against a person or thing.

ego - Anything that makes you feel less than Divine is the ego. That part of us that keeps us separate from all.

equanimity - Equal, even; not too happy, not too sad. Equal in the mind.

fruit of your action - Wanting a reward, or expecting a return, for things you do or say. All things should be dedicated to God. He is the real Doer, we the instruments.

Karma - Karma, or perhaps destiny, is created by ourselves through our actions, either in this life or others. The word also refers to the actions themselves, as well as their consequences. Cause and effect. Action and reaction.

liberated - To set free. To release, to remove old ways.

motives - Something that makes a person act a certain way.

That which moves a person. The goal or object of one's actions.

> Example: A baby wanders into the street and the parents rush out, grab the child and say, "NO!". The baby knows his parents are not happy with him and he starts to cry. The action is the parents rushing to the street, telling the baby, "NO!". The motivation was not to make the child cry, but to teach and assure future safety.

reincarnation - Rebirth of the soul in a new body. The belief that upon death of the body, the soul moves to a different body or form.

senses - Sight, hearing, touch, smell and taste. A receiving of impressions by these five senses keeps us busy fulfilling their wishes.

values - Worth, importance. The worth of something as measured against other things. To regard highly. To consider with respect. Also, rules to live by that encourage right conduct.